Published in 2017, shortly after

the swifts migrated from England.

This book was independently published by Chirpy Stories Ltd,

a micro children's picture book publishing company.

Text Copyright © 2017 Jonathan Walker

Illustrations Copyright © 2017 Jonathan Walker

Jonathan would like to say a special thank you to Lisa Zahn, the copyeditor.
Lisa also provided encouragement to proceed with the publication of this book.

ISBN 978-1-9997606-0-1 Hardback
ISBN 978-1-9997606-1-8 Softback

Bill and the little Red Plane

Written by Jonathan Walker & Illustrated by Rosaria Costa

This book is dedicated to my son, Reuben Peter Walker.
May Reuben, like Bill, have a sense of wonder in God's creation
and seek answers to the natural world around him.

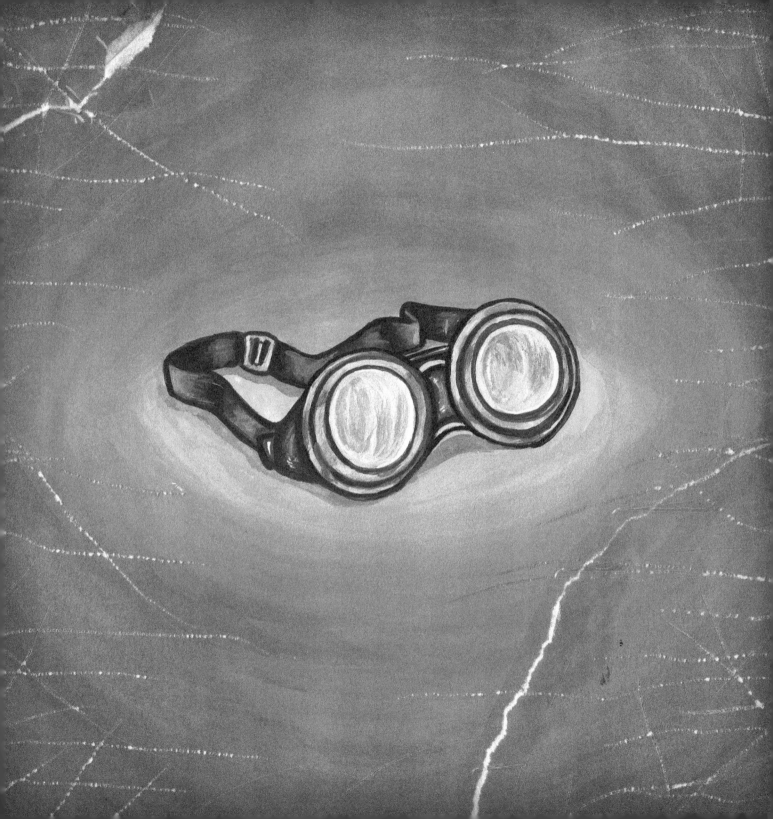

It was a bright and sunny late summer morning, and Bill was playing in the garden.

He looked up and saw a flock of swifts dancing in the sky.

Bill watched in wonder.
He was curious to know where the swifts were flying.

Just then, Bill heard the roar of an engine.
It was a little red plane!
The pilot saw him and waved.
Bill returned the wave and smiled.
The pilot looked so happy in his little red plane.

Suddenly, the plane climbed higher
and higher into the sky.
The plane started to lean backwards.
It went upside down.
Then it dived
before levelling out.

The pilot had done
a loop the loop!

WOOD

Bill ran into the kitchen speechless.

He had never seen a stunt like that before.
The plane had disappeared over the horizon,
in the same direction as the swifts.

Bill told his parents all about it.

Then they sat down and enjoyed a breakfast
of blueberry pancakes with honey,
fresh coffee, and orange juice.
It tasted yummy.

After breakfast, Bill's dad said,

"Okay everyone, grab your coats,
shoes, and camera.
We're off on a mystery tour."

Bill bubbled with excitement at his dad's words.
His mum sat and watched with a loving smile.
The family put their coats and shoes on,
got into the car, and drove off.

Bill still didn't know where they were going.

They travelled past
his school
and kept going.

They passed
his church
and kept going.

They passed
his best
friend's house
and still kept going.

They were now
in the countryside,
with fields
and hedgerows
and trees all around.

Suddenly, a bright windsock caught Bill's attention.

Bill's dad parked the car.
They walked toward a strange, metal building.
Bill couldn't contain himself anymore.
He tried to rush ahead.
He longed to know where they were.

He saw a long, wide piece of road
that stretched far into the distance,
and then ended.

Bill thought this was an odd place.

Inside the metal building
was the little red plane and the pilot.

His mum motioned for Bill to talk to the pilot.

"Hello, Mr Pilot, sir," said Bill.

"You can call me Edward. Today is a special day.
You and I are going flying," he said with a warm
smile.

Filled with joy, Bill ran towards his parents
and hugged them and thanked them.

Bill put on the special flying goggles and jumped into the little red plane.
Edward climbed into the pilot's seat.

"Chocks away!"
exclaimed Edward as he fired up the engine.

The plane rolled forward and left the hangar.
Everything now made sense.
It was not a road he had seen earlier.
It was a runway.

And the strange metal building was an aircraft hangar.
The plane moved faster and faster as it zoomed down the runway.

They zipped past the bright windsock wafting in the breeze and lifted off the ground.

Edward turned to face Bill.
"Where would you like to fly?" asked Edward.
Bill thought about where he would like to go.
He saw another flock of swifts and remembered.

I want to know where the swifts go, he thought.
"Follow those swifts, please," replied Bill.

"Okay," said Edward.
"This will be an adventure."

The swifts were heading south.
It seemed like they were on a mission.
Bill and Edward were excited to see
where this flight would take them.

They both loved a mystery and an adventure,
and this would be great fun!

The plane was now behind the swifts.
Together, they swooped above farmland,
swooshed over buildings,
whizzed past Bill's house,
and swirled above Bill's favourite park.

The park was full of people enjoying a picnic.

Bill and Edward were now heading into
unknown territory. The mystery deepened.
They could see the sea,
and they were moving toward it.
As they soared above the cliffs,
families were eating ice cream, flying kites,
and building sandcastles on the beach below.

Further and further they flew. France was near, and the swifts pressed on.

They didn't seem tired at all. Bill and Edward could see farmers working in the vineyards, picking grapes.

Onward they drifted, still heading south.
Spain was not far away.
Bill was so glad he had his beloved camera with him.

Over Spain, they floated.
Bill had never been so far from home.
The birds kept going.

Edward was beginning to wonder how far this quest would take them.
Another sea appeared, the Mediterranean.
Beyond that, lay Africa!

They both fizzed
with excitement about Africa.
Below them now was the desert.
Camels were wandering
across sand dunes.

Eventually, the desert
gave way to grasslands.

Bill saw a giraffe! The giraffe was chomping on leaves.

Then Bill saw hippos rolling in mud,
and an elephant stomping.

Yet these small garden birds kept flying.

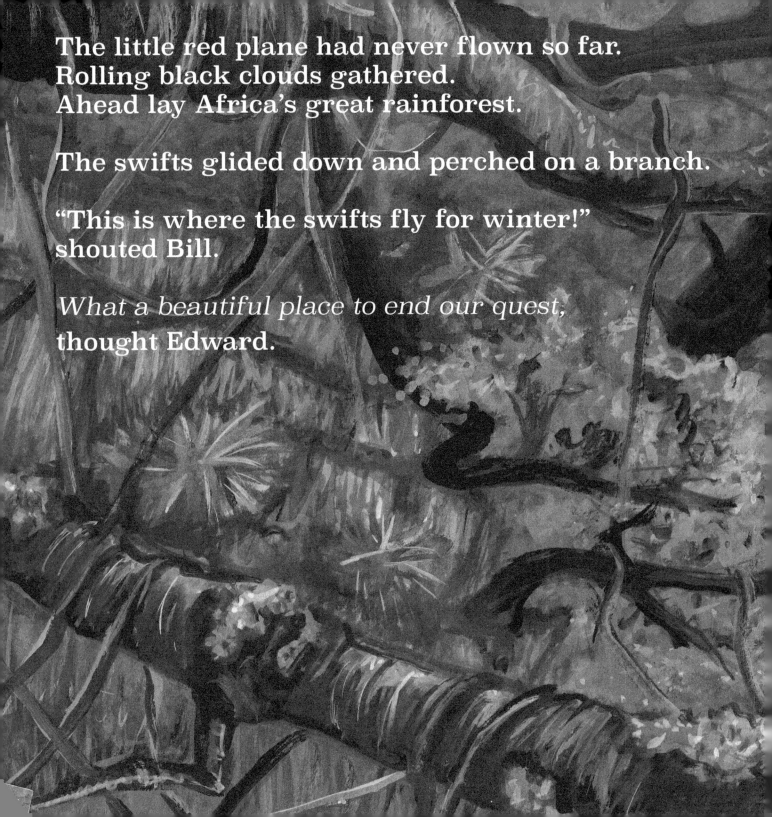

The little red plane had never flown so far.
Rolling black clouds gathered.
Ahead lay Africa's great rainforest.

The swifts glided down and perched on a branch.

"This is where the swifts fly for winter!"
shouted Bill.

What a beautiful place to end our quest,
thought Edward.

It was time to make
the long journey home.
It was now winter
in England,
and few birds remained.
Most had flown south.

The plane landed with
a gentle bump.

Bill and Edward enjoyed
a glass of lemonade
and a slice
of gooey chocolate cake.
It was the perfect way
to finish
an epic adventure!

Bill thanked Edward
for such
a memorable time
and said goodbye.

That night, Bill went to bed with a sense of awe.

The world is huge.
Yet those small birds flew across it.

Bill looked forward to seeing the swifts again in
spring.

Just as he was falling asleep,
he wondered something.

*How did the swifts find their way
to Africa and back?*

Nobody knows. Another mystery!

Swift fun facts

Swifts eat bugs mid-flight
and collect up to 1,000 bugs at a time.
They turn the bugs into balls using saliva,
and the ball is called a bolus.

They need all those bugs
to fuel their long journeys
so they can fly hundreds of miles a day!

Chemicals used by farmers
to protect crops
kill the bugs that swifts eat.

Swifts can drink rain as it falls,
and scoop water from lakes
without landing.

At level flight, no bird is faster than a swift.
They can reach 69.3 miles per hour.
That is as fast as a car on a motorway!

Nobody knows how swifts navigate on their annual
migration.

Swifts spend their whole lives with one mate.
Swifts fly up to 10,000 feet to avoid predators—nearly
as high as the giant volcano, Mt. Etna, in Sicily!

Swifts do all the above, yet weigh only 45 grams,
about the weight of a chocolate bar!

For more information, visit https://www.rspb.org.uk/.

ABOUT THE AUTHOR

Jonathan lives in Hampshire, England, with his wife, Anna, and son, Reuben. Jonathan is a man of faith who relishes the joys of God's creation.

ABOUT THE ILLUSTRATOR

Rosaria Costa was born in Agrigento in 1991,
and she now lives and works in Siculiana, Sicily.
She graduated from the Academy of Fine Arts in Catania,
specialising in picture books and children's illustrations.

https://rosariacosta.carbonmade.com

Lightning Source UK Ltd.
Milton Keynes UK
UKHW05f0845100918
328633UK00006B/72/P